Dear Parents:

Congratulations! Your child is taking the first steps on an exciting journey. The destination? Independent reading!

STEP INTO READING® will help your child get there. The program offers five steps to reading success. Each step includes fun stories and colorful art or photographs. In addition to original fiction and books with favorite characters, there are Step into Reading Non-Fiction Readers, Phonics Readers and Boxed Sets, Sticker Readers, and Comic Readers—a complete literacy program with something to interest every child.

Learning to Read, Step by Step!

Ready to Read   Preschool–Kindergarten
• big type and easy words • rhyme and rhythm • picture clues
For children who know the alphabet and are eager to begin reading.

Reading with Help   Preschool–Grade 1
• basic vocabulary • short sentences • simple stories
For children who recognize familiar words and sound out new words with help.

Reading on Your Own   Grades 1–3
• engaging characters • easy-to-follow plots • popular topics
For children who are ready to read on their own.

Reading Paragraphs   Grades 2–3
• challenging vocabulary • short paragraphs • exciting stories
For newly independent readers who read simple sentences with confidence.

Ready for Chapters   Grades 2–4
• chapters • longer paragraphs • full-color art
For children who want to take the plunge into chapter books but still like colorful pictures.

STEP INTO READING® is designed to give every child a successful reading experience. The grade levels are only guides; children will progress through the steps at their own speed, developing confidence in their reading.

Remember, a lifetime love of reading starts with a single step!

To Ceiba and Sol
—C.I.M.

Visit us on the Web!
StepIntoReading.com
randomhousekids.com

Educators and librarians, for a variety of teaching tools, visit us at RHTeachersLibrarians.com

ISBN 978-1-5247-1696-7 (trade) — ISBN 978-1-5247-1697-4 (lib. bdg.)

Printed in the United States of America

10 9 8 7 6 5 4 3 2 1

by C. Ines Mangual

based on the teleplay "Hundred Mile Race"
by Halcyon Person

illustrated by Kevin Kobasic

Random House 🏠 New York

Vroom!

Blaze has turned
into a race car.
He is ready to roll!

Fender, Dash, and Rally
are ready, too.
They smile and wave
to their fans.

Crusher

also wants to join

the race.

No pushing, Crusher!

Ready. Set. Go!

The racers take off.

Vroom! Vroom!

Crusher is in the lead.

But Blaze catches up!

Crusher wants to cheat.

He uses a

Giant Coconut Blaster

to slow down Blaze

and the other racers!

Oh, no!
The coconuts
block the track!

Blaze uses

a super-strong cutter

to slice the coconuts.

Go, Blaze, go!

Zoom!

Blaze and his friends
speed down the track
after Crusher.

Crusher has
a new plan.
He races into
a dark cave!

Crusher makes
a robot spider
to stop Blaze.

Oh, no!
The spider
traps Blaze and AJ
in a giant web!

They are stuck!
What can they
use to break free?

Blaze has an idea.
He turns himself
into a Super-Spreader
Monster Machine!

Blaze rips through
the web!
He leads the racers
out of the tunnel.

Crusher is still
far ahead.

Blaze uses Blazing Speed
and wins the race!

Hooray for Blaze
and all his fast friends!